This book belongs to

....

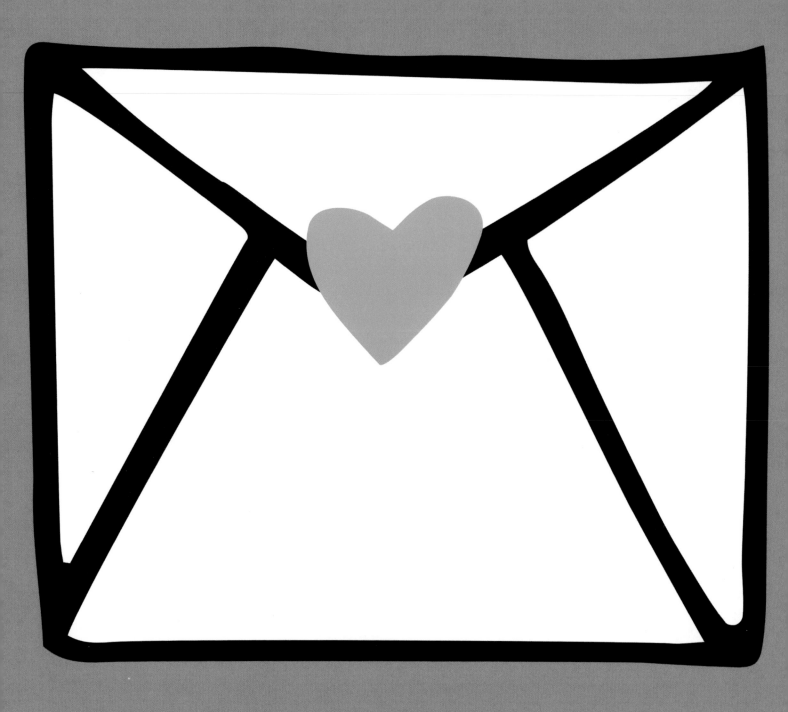

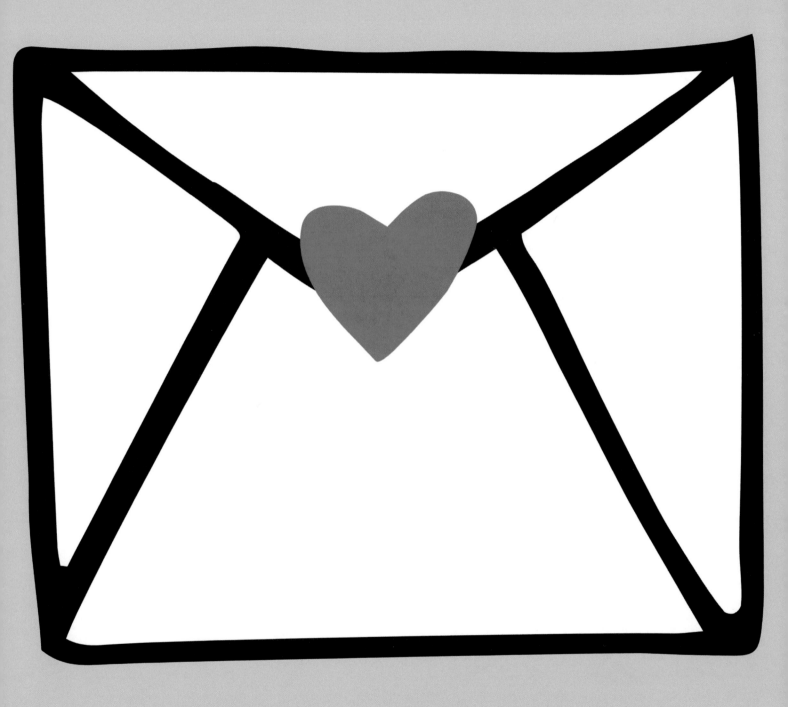

Logan is busy making Valentine's Day cards for all his dino friends.

He is using his favorite pens and lots of red glitter.

He wants to make sure that all his friends know exactly how much he cares about them and why they are so special.

He loves Topsy because he is so creative.
He can make anything using junk and it still turns out beautiful.

He always paints the
mountains so amazingly.

He loves Violet because she is super fast.
She can catch anything.

She always comes first in every race.

He loves Cole because he is the best at telling jokes.
He can make anything seem funny.

Cole always makes Logan laugh even if he is feeling down.

He loves Angie because she is adventurous. She can make anything seem like an exciting adventure.

She always discovers new things for the little dinos to see and do.

He loves Mendal because he is the wisest dinosaur in the land.

He can tell you anything you need to know.

He always has the best advice and the best parties.

He loves Peri because he is a superstar baker. He can make anything out of the most random ingredients.

He always has the tastiest treats in town.

Logan is super excited to give his valentines out
to all his friends.

He puts a special sticker on the envelope of each one.

There is a knock on the cave door. *Who could that be?* he thinks to himself.

"Surprise! Happy Valentine's!"
shout all the dinosaurs.

They love Logan because he is the most caring dinosaur.

He would do anything for the dinosaurs he loves. He always makes sure that everyone feels welcome and loved.

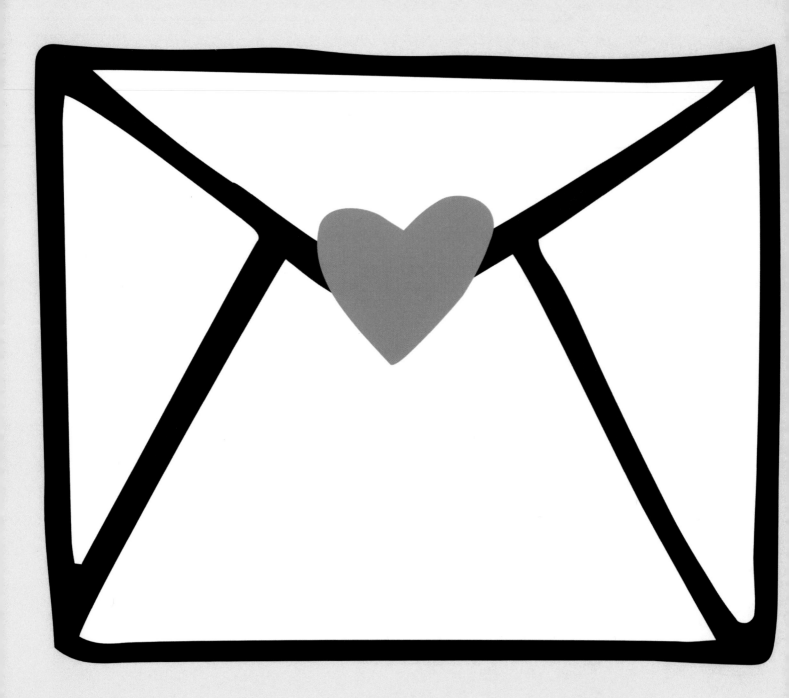

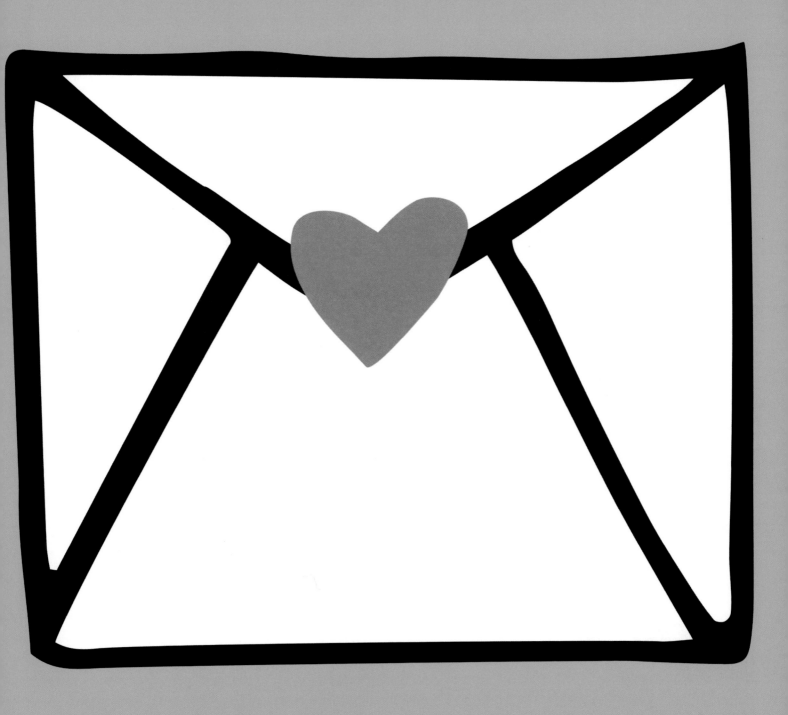

If you have enjoyed this book, please leave a review on Amazon.
It has a significant impact on independent creatives like myself.

Thank you so much!

Jessica Brady

THE DINOSAURS HALLOWEEN ADVENTURE

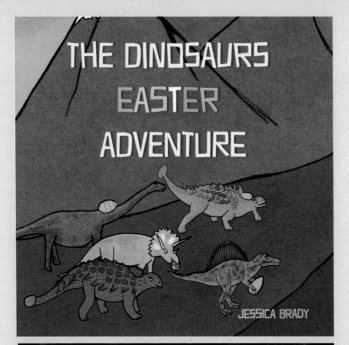

THE DINOSAURS EASTER ADVENTURE

JESSICA BRADY

THE DINOSAURS ST. PATRICKS DAY

COMING
MID-FEBRUARY
2020.

The Dinosaurs Chinese New Year Adventure

Jessica Brady

Made in the USA
Monee, IL
11 February 2022

91098661R00019